About the Author

Darren Neaves was born in 1988 in Margate, Kent.
He always enjoyed fantasy adventure films and video
games during his childhood and teen years.
In later years he enjoyed reading fantasy, Sci-fi and horror
books. He began writing in 2017.
He works for the NHS, supports marine conservation, and
also enjoys reading history and mythology.

The Wizardry World of Walterwitz

Darren Neaves

The Wizardry World of Walterwitz

Olympia Publishers
London

www.olympiapublishers.com
OLYMPIA PAPERBACK EDITION

A CIP catalogue record for this title is
available from the British Library.

ISBN: 978-1-80074-099-0

This is a work of fiction.
Names, characters, places and incidents originate from the writer's
imagination. Any resemblance to actual persons, living or dead, is
purely coincidental.

First Published in 2021

Olympia Publishers
Tallis House
2 Tallis Street
London
EC4Y 0AB

Printed in Great Britain

Crystalex

Walterwitz the wizard lived on a large mountain called Cloud Mountain in a large white castle. Nearby, on a mountain above a city called Tintown lived Crystalex the dragon. The people of Tintown could live happy, normal lives, but threats and dangers from the dragon were always a possibility. Walterwitz the wizard would be on guard and look out for any signs of trouble. He was never seen without his little hat and robe, which were grey and purple, or his sword and his wizard staff. When he had the time, he would visit children and take them on exciting adventures. Also, he would visit Tintown and say hello to people and would voluntarily do community work. Most people were happy to see Walterwitz, especially the children, as he would show them magic. Some adults didn't know what to make of the man with his funny clothes and staff, and the stories he would tell children about magic, beasts and creatures.

'Did I tell you about the time I met a big ugly troll?' he would say to them. 'Or when I saved people's lives with the power of my staff?'

One afternoon, in the market square of Tintown, some children gathered around to see Walterwitz and he told them about when he was a child and his wizard father took him out to see the wildlife of a forest.

'I saw many colourful birds, butterflies and many animals that I didn't recognise. My father was standing on a cliff edge enjoying the view, as I saw wolf staring at me. I told my father, and he said "It's because you're a young wizard. We are different from the other people around here." Then we moved along. I looked down at the river below. There were some children throwing rocks in it. We then headed down to the riverside. The children were no longer there when we got to the river. My father sat on a large rock, holding his staff. I looked at its end, where it was shining and glowing colours in the sunlight. Suddenly, it sparkled, making me jump, and my father laughed. I wanted to have a staff like his. He told me I will when I'm ready.'

'I want magic powers too!' said a boy.

'Yeah,' said the other children.

'Maybe one day you will,' said Walterwitz.

'What did you do first when you became a big wizard?' asked a girl.

'I went for a peaceful walk one warm and quiet evening. I saw children playing at the top of a cliff. I thought they would have an accident if not careful, and then they did. I saw a boy suddenly fall off the cliff. I reached out my staff, then, using its magical force, I landed him to safety. I told them it was getting late and they should start heading for home, or their parents would get worried and cross. Then I said the night monsters will be coming out.'

'What are night monsters?' asked a boy called Charlie.

'They are monsters that come out at night, Charlie,' said Walterwitz.

'Monsters aren't real,' said another girl.

'Yes, they are,' said a boy. 'I've seen a big one, flying around in the sky.'

'Maybe it was a bird or dragon,' said the girl.

'Dragons are not real, are they?' asked Charlie.

'Yes, I had a fight with a dragon,' said the other boy. 'And a troll who wanted to eat me.'

'Are you sure about that?' asked Walterwitz.

'Yes sir. I saved my family from them.'

'I see. Well done, boy. I saw a troll for the first time when I was your age. It was in a cave and my father went to warn him about scaring and stealing from people. But they are rather grumpy, stubborn creatures, who wouldn't listen. So my father turned him into a dwarf troll. He couldn't push his weight around so much after that.'

Then a big bang went off, followed by frantic screams in the distance. Walterwitz headed down the road in that direction, where, further down, he saw what were once houses, now reduced to rubble and ruins. Amongst the crowd of people was a shouting, hysterical, elderly gentleman.

'All is lost! The brutal beast! Curses, I knew this day would come.'

'What happened?' Walterwitz asked as he approached the gent, who leaned on a guard's shoulder.

The guard replied to Walterwitz. 'The dragon, they say. I heard and saw a load of chaos and carnage, But no dragon myself.'

A young man approached Walterwitz. 'It was a dragon, sir. I saw it coming — it came in through the wall, looked around, and then went straight on through the other wall. Seemed to be searching for something.'

'What it wants or what it's up to, I don't want to know, but I probably should.'

'Indeed, Mr Walterwitz,' said the elderly gentleman.

9

'I've had my fair share of this kind during my lifetime.'

Walterwitz looked around in the sky. 'It's probably gone back to its cave. I'll go see what I can find.'

'Let me come too,' said the guard.

'Very well, but stay alert.'

As they reached the end of the dusty long road, they headed up the mountainside. Walterwitz looked at the guard.

'We're about half way now, Jason. I don't know if you're much trained in facing such deadly and unpredictable enemies.'

'I'll be fine,' said Jason.

The sun was setting as the evening approached. It started to get cold and windy, but they were also walking up a mountain. Jason seemed to have something on his mind, as he could see the top of the mountain.

'Crystalex, they refer to the dragon as, isn't it? Always known to have an interest in jewels. Or greed, some would say. Perhaps he's looking for treasure. I can't think why he would expect to find much at the home of senior people, though.'

'Best not to think about it so much, Mister Jason. Common thievery may be too simple for this cunning creature. He could be trying to cause a distraction, set a trap, or provoke.'

All was quiet as they approached the cave. Walterwitz headed inside, 'He could be hiding, expecting visitors and then pounce when ready. Or snuggled up taking a nap, or enjoying whatever he may now have. Either way, we shan't be welcome.'

Jason pulled out his sword, looking around at the high

walls. On the right-hand side, there was a large amount of rock by the wall. There was enough space to walk in between. Walterwitz came to the end of cave, which was in shadows. He felt along the walls and ground for anything to hold or feel. 'Is this it?' Jason asked. Walterwitz didn't answer. He thought to himself that there was nothing obvious to go by. Maybe there was another cave entrance around the mountain. They went back outside. Nothing could be seen from there. For now, there was seemingly nothing to do. Crystalex was somewhere out there. Maybe he had another hiding place or was lurking somewhere in Tintown. Rather reluctantly, Walterwitz went home.

That evening, he sat in his big comfy armchair with a bowl of hot soup and smoked his pipe. It's a filthy habit that wizards should be a bit wiser about. But Walterwitz admittedly took quite a pleasure from it, on a cold night, anyway. He sipped his soup whilst thinking about the day. Was there something he overlooked? Did he really do everything he could? He decided to have a little nap. But he actually stayed asleep through the night. He woke just after sunrise, rather surprised that he slept through the night in his chair. Once he had a hot bath and washed his robe, he had his breakfast. Then he went to town.

Much of the mess left by the dragon had been cleared up. But then the dragon was seen flying in circles around the city. It was high up, but it was him all right. Walterwitz could see it was, and that he went off towards the mountain. Once again, Walterwitz went after him. He entered the cave where the wild beast was believed to live. But just like the day before, it was just a bare cave. He went behind the rock. Then a big rumbling noise filled the cave. As Walterwitz peered out behind the rock, Crystalex came stomping past, muttering to himself as he walked outside. Through the secret doorway, Walterwitz could see a glow in the distance, and then the door shut suddenly. He went outside to where the dragon had gone. He couldn't see anything in the sky, so he stepped forward to look over the hillside.

'Boo!' Crystalex went as he snuck up behind Walterwitz. 'This is a rather unusual place for a silly old wizard to be lurking. Are you lost?' The dragon asked whilst glaring intently.

'It's your mind that's lost! If it was ever there in the first place.'

'Oh, nasty, grumpy old man, silly, beardy old man.'

Walterwitz pointed his staff at the dragon's snout, which was getting closer to his face. 'You keep lurking around the city. Been looking for something, haven't you? Anything besides trouble? You should look for something to pay for the damage and harm you've caused.'

Crystalex sat down and sighed. 'Always calling me trouble, you are. Very rude and unfair of you. I try to be nice to everyone, but you keep telling lies to all the stupid children. They're the real troublesome ones. They spread nasty stories. More than ever now, thanks to old Walley-witz wizard.'

Walterwitz stepped forward. 'You destroyed people's homes, that's the sort of thing that makes people call you trouble. Now you will be held responsible for your actions.'

Crystalex took a breath. 'Oh, so I did. I am very sorry about that.'

'You will be if you don't clear up your act, and give back to the folks of Tintown.'

'Of course. But I'm going through a difficult time right now. A priceless family treasure is lost and it's very upsetting for us all. That reminds me, I must get back to searching.'

'Stay away from the city! You've done enough searching there. Or treasures will be the least of your worries.'

'Why, old wizard, must you make threats to someone who's going through enough trouble as it is? I said you were nasty and grumpy. I've said I am sorry for upsetting the people.'

'Well, maybe one of your treasures can be used to pay what you owe. I'm sure you have plenty.'

'Oh yes, yes, I will be able to pay, but not this very minute, you must understand.'

'Fine, I shall report back to the king. I'm sure we will all be expecting to see you again soon.'

In the centre of Tintown there was a big gathering of people rather startled by recent events and gossiping about what could happen next. Some were awfully afraid, others were just angry. The king stepped out of his palace door towards the crowd. They hadn't even noticed that their king was standing right there. He looked at them all from left to right, wondering what he could possibly do with such a bunch. He then raised his hand, trying to get some attention.

'Silence!' he shouted. Few heard him. Some turned to face him, others soon followed. Again, the king demanded, 'Can I have your attention, please!'. One of the peasants looked at the king with a confused look.

'You're not doing lunch today, are you?'

'Silence you dolt!' snapped the king. 'I understand the

concerns that many of you may have. Please try to stay calm, that's the smart thing to do.'

They all just nodded willingly and quietly.

'Good people, we have always tried to make ourselves prepared for any trouble and deadly situation, and I'm sure all my men and myself can make all well for us all'.

Walterwitz arrived to see the king. There was some gentle clapping from the crowd as he approached.

'Walterwitz will save us,' someone shouted out.

The wizard approached the king and bowed. 'Your grace, I don't think Crystalex will attack the city again, but it is of course a possibility. We must make ourselves more prepared in future.'

As he explained to the king his meeting with the dragon and his explanation for his havoc, the crowd surrounded them listening in.

'I'm not interested in any excuses from that vile creature. He deserves to be destroyed.'

'Yes, your grace, but I think it's unwise to just go angrily after the dragon on some wild goose chase.'

'What geese are there around here?' asked the peasant.

Walterwitz frowned at him. 'Silence, you dolt!'

A few days had passed and there was no sight or sound of Crystalex. The king was sitting in his chair while two of his guards were playing draughts. Finally, fed up with waiting, the king ordered the guards to go and gather all the other guards. 'Okay men, it's time to get the dragon and have justice served.'

Twenty of the palace guards were aligned, the king checked that they all had their best weaponry and armour. He then led the guards out of the palace, through the town centre and out into the woods.

'Now go and find the biggest, most powerful tree trunk and chop it down.'

The guards split into four groups of five and searched the entire woods to find a big and sturdy tree. Jason the guard was in the group that came across what looked as if it was certainly the best tree for them.

'Your grace!' Jason called out. He then called to the other guards and they all gathered around the big tree.

'Okay men, I'm sure you can handle this, knock it down so we have our battering ram.'

'Holding up their big strong axes, the guards chopped away at the tree. The king stood there encouraging, or commanding them: 'Come on! Harder!'.

It was a difficult job despite the strength of the men and their tools. It was also a strong tree, but they soon got it down on the ground with a thundering whack. The king was ready for more of his orders.

'Good,' he said. 'Now we must chop off all the branches, so they don't get in our way.'

So the guards quickly chopped off the branches and with their hard work and loyalty, the battering ram was soon ready. It was now time to carry the trunk out of the woods. Even with ten guards on each side, with their combined strength it was a tough task. They stopped in the middle of the market and it was clear they were getting tired. Some ladies gathered around offering the men water, which they gratefully drank up. Some other men came along to help carry the tree trunk. Jason then started to sound doubtful towards the king.

'I've been to the cave with the secret door. I'm not sure

if this will work.'

'Oh, it will, we shall make it so!'

Once they reached the cave the king called out for the dragon. 'This is your last chance to come along peacefully and obey your king!' he shouted. But all was quiet. 'Very well you silly, foolish, and vile creature! All get ready, men.'

He directed the guards as they stood ready. The king gave them the order to charge and ram the door, which was no longer so secret. All men charged fast and hard with the trunk, ramming it against the door, then backing up and ramming again. So far nothing had happened. No sign of Crystalex or the door being destroyed, as they kept ramming it with all their might. Slowly the trunk was chipping away, then they dropped it to catch their breath. The king was getting frustrated.

'Curses!' he went. 'We must find something stronger. If we could get a ram built from iron or something, it might work. If I go back to my palace, can I trust that it will be taken care of?'

'Yes, your grace,' said the guards.

So the king went to his palace to rest. All the standing around watching his men doing a load of hard work made him feel rather tired.

The next morning, the iron ram was ready and the guards were waiting with it outside the palace. When the king approached the guards, he looked at them and the battering ram.

'Good job, gentlemen! Now to the mountain, march!'

The king's men were doing well with little rest and sleep lately, and all the hard work they had to do. Once they get into that lair and capture Crystalex, it will all be fine, they thought. They arrived at the cave and charged at the door in the cave. They rammed it hard, over and over again. But it still didn't seem to be helping.

'It's not going to break it down and we are all very tired and overworked,' said a guard.

'Maybe Walterwitz could find a way of opening it,' said Jason.

'I am in charge of this land, not some wizard,' the king went.

'Walterwitz has magic and knowledge of dragon ways,' said another guard.

The king got angry. 'I know dragons well enough, thank you very much! Another word and I shall have you executed.'

Walterwitz was visiting the market and talked to one of the traders there. 'Anything interesting today?'

'Nothing special today. Although, watching the king make his men carry a tree trunk through town was something. They must be after the dragon.'

'I see. Maybe I shall go and see how they are doing.'

The king was feeling fed up and powerless. 'I knew all dragons should have been destroyed a long time ago!'

The guards were given a break for a while. Then Walterwitz arrived. 'Maybe I could be of some assistance' he said.

'Very well,' said the king.

Walterwitz approached the door and then held his staff out in front, pointing at the door. Then it suddenly opened.

'That was impressive,' said a guard.

'I didn't do anything yet,' said Walterwitz. 'What! The door just opened itself? After all our hard work?' went the king, angrily. 'All done on purpose by the dragon, no doubt! Trouble making and wasting my precious time, well no more.'

The king stormed through the doorway, down the steps to the bottom. Sunlight was coming in through a load of holes and cracks in the walls, filling the room with enough light to see. The room was big, bare and empty. There was no sign of the dragon here or even any trace of one. Walterwitz looked up to the top of the cave where it was dark. He held up his staff and shot a bolt of lightning up to the top, lightning it up. There was nothing there. No dragon, it was clear to all, but no one said anything.

The king was almost red with rage. 'Find me that damn beast!' he commanded. 'Bring me his treasure too! Or whatever he may have. Whatever it is, he doesn't deserve it and it should all be mine!'

Walterwitz was still in the centre of the room as the king left, followed by the palace guards. He closed his eyes and tried to envision where the dragon was. Nothing. He tried again. Still couldn't see anything. He walked out of the mountain thinking he probably should have never let the dragon out of his sight. Like he was going to just happily accept his punishment. 'Oh, you big fool,' he thought.

As he approached the city, the boy Charlie came up to him. 'Have you got the dragon yet?'

'Not yet, Charlie.' 'I'm sure you will soon.'

The next day, the king sat, grumpily, in his chair. Then the maid came in the room.

'Bring me wine, Woman!'

'Yes, your grace,' she replied. Soon she was there at his side with a glass and bottle, and then she poured him some.

He gulped it straight down.

'More!' he said. She filled his glass up again. He then gulped it down again.

'You may go now,' he told her.

He stayed sitting in his chair. Totally unaware that word was going around that a big, fire-breathing dragon had destroyed the nearby town of Winton, burning every building to cinders and killing many people, and leaving many more homeless and very afraid without a clue what to do with themselves.

George, the guard, entered the room and marched up to report to the king. 'Your grace, word is going around that a big, fire breathing dragon has destroyed the nearby town of Winton, burning every building to cinders and killing many people, and leaving many more homeless and very afraid without a clue what to do with themselves.'

The king stood straight up. 'Bye George!'

'Are you talking to me, or expressing yourself?'

'Silent boy!' The king turned around to the big window. He could see the big cloud of smoke. 'I see. Now, we must not let this happen here! I want everyone on guard to fight off any approaching dragon.'

Everyone in Tintown heard the news and were as ready as they could be. Some closed and locked all their doors and windows and hid silently in their homes. Other people were on their roofs with bow and arrows. Ohers stood by with hose pipes and buckets of water. Walterwitz had his sword and staff, full of all the mightiness of a good wizard. The wizard, king and palace guards were outside the palace.

'Where is that stupid pinkie, purple dragon thing,' said the king. 'He signed his death warrant long ago. Now it's far beyond that. Oh, what a nerve and liberty!'

'It may not be Crystalex, your grace. There are other dragons about,' Walterwitz replied.

'Doesn't matter! I want them all destroyed. Turn them all into a bonfire, like they deserve. What a ridiculous look and colour for a dragon. I mean, they are stupid anyway. But if he had a nice, bright red or green colour, it may look rather nice and smart. But no, he has to have that colour. Probably just to annoy me. But it won't work I tell you! Oh, I wish the damn thing would hurry up and show itself so I can roast it. Yes, we can have dragon for dinner.'

Walterwitz turned to face the king. 'I don't think that would be good idea your grace. Dragons aren't meant for eating.'

'No, I guess not. Too worthless to be any good, even in death.' The king turned to Walterwitz. 'I know you wear purple, but you manage to pull it off. It looks smart on you.'

'Thank you, your grace.'

'That dragon is mine. Only one thing can get in my way now.'

'What's that?' asked Walterwitz.

'That idiot writer, or creator, making me just sit around doing nothing, rather than being heroic and having my moment.'

'Isn't Walterwitz supposed to be the hero around here?' asked Jason.

'Silence with your nonsense!' Went the king. 'Yes, Walterwitz is a good man and has done great things for us all. But I'm king, and I shall have the fame and rewards that I deserve. I shall get what I want, and no kind of creator will stop me.'

Then there was a big puff of smoke, and then standing there was Shadowitz, the black wizard, who, using his wizard ways, took the king inside the palace and to his chair. Then taught him the valuable lesson, that being a rich, powerful and important king, is all very well and good, but he should still know how and when to keep his mouth shut.

Walterwitz then looked down the road, and he could hardly believe his eyes as Crystalex seemed to be lying by the road. Then the guards soon noticed too. Then, led by Walterwitz, they slowly and carefully walked down towards the dragon. He seemed to be sleeping, so they all surrounded him. With their swords pointing right at him so he couldn't escape. Then Crystalex woke up to the wizard's mighty blade.

'Leave me in peace.'

'Silence,' said Walterwitz. 'What are you doing here? Was it you who destroyed that town?'

'No, I wouldn't do a thing like that.'

'I find that hard to believe, and you haven't paid up as we agreed. Instead, you just disappeared for a while. Now you're just having a nap in the road. We have had enough of your games.'

'I have had a very hard time lately and I haven't even had any time to go to bed. Then when I finally try, you nasty people start to bully me again.'

'Everybody knows a horrid dragon burned down the town of Winton. If it wasn't you, then who was it?'

'I don't know! Not me. I can't breathe fire, I've never been able to. Other dragons used to make fun of me when I was little and I'm still being bullied by you nasty, silly people, from a silly city with a silly fool of a king and wizard.'

'Hang on,' said one of the guards. 'Didn't people say it was a white dragon that attacked Winton?'

'Now you mention it, I did hear that.' Said another guard.

'Not Diamondox, the great white?' Walterwitz asked.

'What?' asked Jason.

'Diamondox the white and large dragon. I have never seen it before, but have read about it. Legend has it that he is master of all dragons.'

'So he is the one pulling the strings around here, and this vile creature is just a tool?' asked Jason.

'Perhaps so,' said Walterwitz. He then told the guards to shackle the dragon's feet together. 'Now, Crystalex, come along with us quietly,' ordered Walterwitz.

They marched down the road, all keeping their eyes on the dragon, and took him into the jailhouse. 'Just try to not cause any more trouble and you may be free to go when I decide to allow it.'

The king came out of the palace after being told what had just happened, just as the guards were entering the square followed by Walterwitz.

'What's all this I hear about Diamondox the black, or Walterwitz the white, or whatever?' asked the king.

'I fear, your grace, that things are worse than we thought. The great white dragon burned down Winton, and most likely controls Crystalex, who we now have safely behind bars. But I don't think anyone knows where Diamondox is or what he's really up to. He may come here to destroy the town or get Crystalex.'

'Curse these damn dragons! If Crystalex doesn't

provide us with anything helpful or useful he shall be killed immediately. He must know what the dragons are up to. I will make him talk if it's the last thing I do.'

'Well, your grace, I could go to my study and find out more about the beast. Find out more about what is known of the white dragon and what we can expect from them all. I can still keep my eyes and ears open for any signs of trouble.'

So Walterwitz went to his castle to do more research on the dragons. Meanwhile, the king had some fun with the other dragon.

'Ah ha ha ha!' went the king as he kicked and poked him with his sceptre. 'I have you now, you stupid little rat. I shall have the fun that I deserve, then when we all have finally had enough you will be put to death! I am your king, and you will obey and fear me!'

While Crystalex was an adult dragon, he was young and small compared to other dragons. He was also shackled, making things difficult for him.

'I don't care for some silly king, you will be sorry. All you nasty, stupid humans will be sorry.'

'Trying to threaten the king is not very wise, you nasty little thing. This is my land, I am the law and I say all stupid dragons are to be destroyed. You will not harm or ruin my people's lives anymore! This is the day Tintown has been waiting for.'

'The people of Tintown are just a bunch of mindless fools.'

'That's not the point. They are people of my land and I am their king. I am a great king. The greatest of all.'

Walterwitz approached the large doors to his castle. He

pulled out a long and shiny, silver key. As he unlocked the doors there was a loud creaking noise. Then there was another one, as he pushed the door open. Once he closed the door behind him, he took to the stairway, which was right of the front door. He reached the top of the stone stairway and went into his study room, which was next to the top of the stairs. The room had several bookshelves stretching from one side to the other, all full of thick books. Half of them were covered in thick dust. They were mostly books that Walterwitz didn't need to go through any more. But he didn't like the thought of getting rid of them. He had to think for a moment, trying to remember which book he was reading when he came across the great dragons. He knew it was one of the blue books. He looked at one of them and grabbed hold of it. 'I think this is the one,' he thought as he took a seat in his old rocking chair. Indeed, it was the book he had in mind. But finding the right section would probably take longer. Then a raven started flying about outside the window, which was open. Then it landed on the window sill. Walterwitz looked at it, it just stood still like a statue, and they just stared at each other.

Now, Crystalex had at least a few minutes of peace to himself. He gently lifted his large tongue and a diamond fell out of his mouth, where he had been hiding them. He was clever and sneaky that way. Maybe he had only just found them before he was captured. Or maybe he was hiding them from Diamondox all along. He looked at his jewels, then he heard approaching footsteps, so he quickly hid them in his mouth again.

When the strange raven decided to bugger off somewhere else, Walterwitz started flicking through his book. He found what he was looking for. He saw a headline that said "Dragon jewels". He started to read: *It has been said throughout time that the most deadly and large dragons keep diamonds, crystals and gems on them when resting in their homes. These are the white, red and green dragons. Not being the type to sell their jewels so they can visit the market, these wild beasts have a natural yet unexplained need to have their jewels close to them while they sleep or relax. Some believe that they keep them near to help them smell or sense prey, or hunters. Legend has it that if a dragon jewel is lost or stolen, they simply go on a rage, burning everything to ashes until their treasure is revealed. The dragon's jewel is about the only thing in the world to not get destroyed, or even damaged by their fire, which may be another reason for their love of the jewels. The diamonds also seem to contain a strange power which was discovered when a child stuck a knife into one of them. Once he pulled it out, the knife was filled with some kind of energy. When a fly landed on it, it gave a shock that killed it. The large white and green dragons, unlike the other dragons, have never been known to speak. Whether this is because they can't, or choose not to, is not known. Dragons are not the easiest of creatures to study alive, or dead. People have rarely had a good chance or the will to.*

Walterwitz then looked up from his book for a little think. Then he noticed that the raven was back. He also noticed how its eye was very bright and sparkly, like a jewel.

'Are you trying to tell me something?'

Again, the raven stood still and silent. Ever since he was a child, he'd had a good bond with animals. But this bird seemed strange even to him. Eventually, he just shouted 'Go away,' and it did so, and never returned.

'We must find those jewels and stop the dragon, if it's not too late already,' Walterwitz thought as he headed back to Tintown.

The king and George came up to the cell. 'This is your last chance to tell us what you know,' said the king. 'I won't have you around unless it's absolutely necessary. Now speak up or you will die. Tell me everything, and then you will only die a bit later. But you will die with slightly more dignity and class. We may even give you a proper burial. Then at least people will know you as a dragon, who wasn't foolish enough to disobey and disrespect his king. A rather nice way to go, wouldn't you say?'

'I have no king and never will, you silly old twit. I am far too superior to such a fool. Any man, really, but a stupid king above all else. Not even the silly people in this city see you as a good leader.'

'Silence!' snapped the king. 'You will not treat me this way, you vile thing! Guard, I demand that the stupid dragon be ready for his burning on the stake as soon as possible. Is that clear?'

'Oh yes your grace. I shall tell all the guards immediately.'

'Good!' went the king with a big grin on his face. 'Yes, I shall treasure and enjoy this day very much. Everyone will come to see the great display. They all shall treasure and enjoy the moment. In the future we all shall mark and remember it with festive events and fun for all, to celebrate the end of the dragon. You dragons won't like the fire I will have for you. I think fire and burning will be a rather fitting way to do it, wouldn't you agree, Crystalex?'

'You won't feel so big and confidant when the other dragons come for you. They will burn you to a crisp! Even all the pee in your pants won't put you out. Nothing can save you! Ah ha ha.'

'You laugh now, but soon you will be crying out in pain.'

Then the king wacked the dragon with his sceptre and walked out. He went to see the guards who were fixing together the stake.

'Nearly all done your grace,' one of them said.

'Good, good, I shall announce the exciting news to the city. The king went to the centre of the town square. 'Ladies and gentlemen, do not go anywhere, as this is a very big and special moment for us all. The death of the dragon is upon us! That's right, and we will all be able to sleep a little easier tonight. This may mean a bit more taxes to pay as we will have a nicer and safer place to live. But well worth it, I think. We shall all enjoy and remember this moment forever.'

The guards all came out carrying the stake. 'Just over here, my good men.' They went over to the king and stood the stake in place. More people started to come over and watch.

The king looked at the guards. 'Now if you could please bring out our guest of honour.'

'Yes, your grace,' said two of the guards, who went to fetch the dragon from his jail. The sky was perfectly clear and blue, and the sun was shining brightly. It was the perfect day for the king to show everyone this moment.

Walterwitz was arriving and went straight to see the

king. 'Ah, dear Walterwitz, nice that you could be here for the big event. That dragon will be of no use to us. So I have rightly decided to finally have it finished. We shall give what it has had coming to it. Our brave people deserve it too.' The guards came out walking the dragon to the stake. 'Make sure he's tied up good and proper. We don't want another dragon on the loose.'

'Your grace, I believe the big dragon is after the diamonds that they have always kept with them. If he can't find them, he will just burn everything in sight until he has found them. We must find them before he gets here.'

'We are well prepared for the dragons. They so much show themselves, I have no doubt you and I can have the damn things destroyed.'

Walterwitz didn't seem to share the king's confidence. 'I'm not sure if even I could stop the dragon from causing any damage and harm. If the diamonds are found first, we can at least spare such destruction and death like what happened in Winton.'

Crystalex was now in place as the guards stepped away. 'Good work men, go and take a nice break in the palace. Walterwitz and I can handle the rest.'

After the king sent the guards away, he said to Walterwitz, 'I don't have a clue about any diamonds. They could only be in the dragon's cave, and we have all searched that for anything. I don't know what to do. Unless you have an idea.'

Walterwitz turned to Crystalex. 'I'm sure you know what your master is up to. Where are the jewels?'

'I will help, if you let me go.'

'Never!' went the king. 'Speak now or you will be

burned awfully slowly and painfully.'

'Well, if you...' then Crystalex closed his mouth. Then started moving his jaw about.

'What are you doing?' went Walterwitz.

'Nothing,' said Crystalex quick and quietly.

'Open your mouth,' Walterwitz said. Slowly, the dragon opened his mouth wide. Then Walterwitz fired a lightning bolt at the dragon's face.

'Ouch!' the dragon cried and the diamonds fell out of his mouth to the floor.

Walterwitz grabbed them fast. 'You had them all the time?'

Walterwitz stood holding the diamonds in his hand. The king was there by his side. Then something could be seen in the sky. It seemed to be getting closer. There were screams as people ran indoors. Diamondox was approaching the city square. Then two men fired their arrows at the dragon. The dragon paused, facing the men, as he grabbed and pulled the arrows out of his side and threw them back towards the men as they ran indoors. The dragon reached the ground and unleashed his breath of fire on their building. Then he turned to face Walterwitz.

The king ran into the palace screaming 'Ah, dragon!'

Walterwitz held out the diamonds, but the dragon did not take any notice of them. He then threw them towards Diamondox. The dragon went towards them. But he still seemed angry. He held up his front paw and tried to strike Walterwitz. The wizard was quick to respond and blocked it with his sword, then held up his staff to strike the dragon with a lightning bolt. That knocked him back. Walterwitz hid behind a pillar of the palace. Jason got out on to the palace roof and peeked over the edge.

'I see you, dragon!'

As the angry Diamondox went over to Walterwitz, hiding behind the pillar he opened his mouth to open fire. Then a splash of water went into his mouth. The dragon shook his head, and then looked upwards where he saw Jason standing there on the roof.

Jason then took out his sword. 'That will slow him down a little,' he shouted.

The dragon then leapt up onto the palace wall, clutching at it with his claws, and started to climb. Jason struck out with his sword.

Walterwitz went over to the jewels. He held out his sword and staff and started a chant. Between the sword and staff, a very bright light appeared. It grew larger quickly and smoothly, until it was as tall as Walterwitz, and then it faded away. Now standing in front of him were the diamonds, but now they were giant diamonds at six feet tall. The dragon had made it to the roof top of the palace where Jason struck with his sword at the paw of Diamondox, making him cry out in pain and anger. Walterwitz fired another bolt of lightning at the dragon, causing him to start losing his grip. Jason slashed out again at the dragon's paw, causing him to fall to the ground with a big thump.

Diamondox lay on the ground, and then turned onto his side. Walterwitz slowly walked to him then the dragon looked up towards the wizard. He then rolled over and got up and fired the most powerful breath of fire he could. Walterwitz hid behind the jewels, and they shielded him from the flames. The angry dragon charged towards the jewels, and then Walterwitz reached out with his staff and zapped his wounded paw, causing him to fall forward, with his head crashing into the diamond. As the dragon lay there dazed, Walterwitz grabbed his sword with both hands and held it high above his head and struck straight into the centre of the nearest jewel. He then yanked to pull the sword out, but it was stuck.

Diamondox tried to clear his head as he got to his feet while Walterwitz shifted and twisted the sword, trying to get it out. He prepared to give it a hard tug, and then he noticed the dragon was there next to him. As he then ran around the jewels, he shot a big blaze of fire. As Diamondox chased him around, Jason threw his sword at the dragon and it went right into his lower back. Diamondox reached to try to pull the sword out of him. As he did that, Walterwitz grabbed hold of his sword, making sure he had a good grip. He pulled and it came out of the jewel with a big shiny glow throughout the blade. Walterwitz held up the sword which he realised was heavier than normal, and it seemed to vibrate, making it harder to hold. Diamondox got a hold of the sword in his back and yanked it out. That was very painful for him. He turned towards Walterwitz, who was approaching him quickly but carefully and gave a good strike through the dragon's neck. A large electrical shock went through his body. He reached up with his paws, and then fell to the ground with a hard thump.

Walterwitz just stood still in awe for a moment as his fallen foe lay still. Jason and a few other people came over. Most of them were just full of relief that the dragon was gone.

'Well done, Walterwitz, and thank you for saving us all,' people said.

Walterwitz looked at Jason. 'Thank you for your assistance, my good fellow. Now, what to do here? We can't have giant diamonds and dragons just lying around.'

'Oh my, the city will be rich. We are all rich,' a man said.

'We could skin him all over. I'm sure there are people local and far away who would buy samples. It could be used as some decoration, or things can be made out of it. The ivory, we could sell to people who visit the city. Now there's no other town nearby, we may start getting more tourists. Unless they get put off by any stories about dragons and anything else unpleasant. People do tend to gossip and spread word about,' Jason went while looking at people around him.

They all looked away at each other shaking their heads and shrugging their shoulders. 'The diamonds, each one would be worth a fortune. They must be the biggest in the world. You are a genius, Walterwitz,' another man said.

'Yes, yes, shall we just try to stay calm and not get over excited,' said Walterwitz.

Jason then said, 'Maybe we should let our hero here decide what to do. He made the diamonds so big and defeated the dragon, we owe him everything.'

The people agreed. A rather flattered Walterwitz went, 'Oh, you can do what you want with the dragon. As Jason said, I'm sure it would be useful for us all.'

'Yes, and all those bones,' a woman said. 'So many of them and so large. They could be good for everybody's dogs.'

'Yes, some of the wildlife would enjoy them too. Like the wolves and bears,' said Jason. 'I guess in one way the dragon was the best thing to happen to the town.'

Walterwitz then looked at Crystalex. 'Do we sell him off to some wealthy people, or chop him up and sell his parts too?' said a man.

'I'm not sure that would really be necessary,' said Walterwitz. He then said to Crystalex, 'If we let you go free and unharmed, and let you have something for yourself, can you be trusted to stay away and out of trouble?'

'Oh, but of course. I don't think I have ever really tried to make trouble for anyone.'

'Can we really trust him?' asked Jason

'Well, he is a somewhat handicapped dragon, and now he is probably the only dragon around. If he does prove to be untrustworthy, we should have no trouble hunting him down.'

'I don't want any trouble. I just want my life and freedom.'

Walterwitz untied Crystalex from the stake, the dragon then stretched his legs and muscles. 'Ooh that's better.'

He then looked at the big diamonds. 'Wow, I rather liked carrying them around with me, but they are much better like that. I used to dream of giant jewels.'

Walterwitz looked at the dragon, thinking that a happy dragon is probably a rather tame and safe dragon to have around. 'I will let you have two of the diamonds and your freedom. If we have the other diamond and our safety.'

'Oh, yes. I don't see humans as much worth the bother. The diamonds will serve me better.'

'Some guards and I will help take the diamonds up to your cave. Jason, you and the rest of the guards can give the other diamond to the king. Tell him that the dragons have been dealt with.'

'Okay then,' said Jason. 'I'm sure the king will be delighted with both the news and the gift.'

The guards and city people worked together to take the great jewels to the dragon's lair and take the last one to the king. He was indeed delighted. No more dragons about, and he soon became well known throughout the kingdom as the man with the biggest diamond that anybody had ever seen. Tourists came to visit the king and the magnificent jewel. They would visit the market which had become more famous with the increasing number of visitors, for its rare gifts and resources.

After Walterwitz and the guards had taken Crystalex to his home with the jewels, they came back to their favourite pub, for a well-earned drink.

'A pint on the house for our heroes,' said the landlord.

After a long day Walterwitz decided to head for home. But he came across the children in the market and sat down and chatted with them for a while. He told them the most amazing story about his encounter with a big dragon.

'The dragon wanted to burn everything!' he told them. 'He loved his diamonds so much that he would destroy everything to get them back. When he found out that I had them, I gave them back to him. But he just wanted to kill me.' The children were amazed. 'I even used my magic to make them much bigger and more valuable. I guess there's just no pleasing some deadly fire breathing dragons.'

So that night, Crystalex slept silently and peacefully in his cave, with his big diamonds. He was all snuggled up with them, and had the most stupid grin on his face.

The father of the cave's residential family of mice came

out to have a good look at the diamonds. He was amazed at what he saw. Both the giant jewels, and the dragon being happy. He ran back inside the hole in the wall.

'He's back,' he said to his wife and two children. 'He has the hugest diamonds. I could never get them in here,' he said as he looked at the small diamond in the corner of the room.

'Why did you take it, anyway?' asked the wife.

'I was hoping I could trade it with the fat mouse down the road. He always gets a lot of good food from somewhere, but he wasn't interested. I took all four diamonds down to him, which was hard work, so I just brought the one back. I guess there's just no pleasing a greedy fat pig.'

'Oh father,' said the daughter. 'He's a mouse, not a pig, you silly old dolt.'

EGLOG

Eglog the troll lived in a cave on a mountainside. These mountains were in fog for most of the year. Eglog lived alone. He was now the only living troll, as far as he knew. His family were separated from him long ago. He was very young at the time, and could never remember there being other troll families around. When he was a child, his home land was taken over by giants. Most of the trolls were eaten or killed, and all the troll's valuables, of which there were very few, were taken. He now lived on the other side of the land, after being forced to flee from his home, far away from the land that he knew. He went off in search of land with trolls and no giants. He did not find any, but he came across a cave to hide in. This was a good cave for Eglog, as it was just big enough for him to fit in and be comfortable. It was also too small for nasty giants to get in, or too near.

Eglog was feeling hungry, so he headed down towards the river to get some fish. It was what he normally did to get some proper food to eat. With the giants either eating up everything, or scaring off everything, it was very hard to find anything else. It was a very misty day. He sat there at the riverbank waiting to get a good fish. There didn't seem to be many about, that he could see.

He remembered being with his father at the river getting a fish, when they were having trouble getting one. He tried to think what it was he did to get one. He eventually had enough of waiting, and tried to find something in the woods. He searched around the woods, but didn't have any more luck there. It was starting to feel that he was the only non-giant left.

'They have taken and destroyed it all.' He was rather hopeful that if they had had everything, the giants would soon starve to death. Years of hatred and quests for revenge, along with hunger, took Eglog to a new level of searching for his food.

'They took everything for themselves and ate up everything themselves.' He carried on, as he knew he would find a place to find food. Then one day he would return to retake what was his.

Just on the outskirt of Tintown was Greenwood farm, owned by farmer Frederson. He was a happy man and was always happy to see friends and people that he met around the town. One morning he stepped outside to feel the morning sunshine on his face. He then saw that one of his ducks was sleeping in the middle of the path, which he had never seen before, and he found it to be very unusual. Indeed, the whole day, or even the week, would prove to be very unusual. He walked over to the duck to see if it was okay. When he got a step away from the duck it suddenly stood straight up and ran off around the corner where the barn was.

'Okay, then,' he said to himself as he went to check the mailbox. It was empty. He then went to the shed to get some food for the pigs. He walked towards the shed to find that it was open. He thought that was very strange. 'I always lock it up,' he thought. Then he saw that the chickens pen was in the messiest state he had ever seen it in, although the chickens were being very still and quiet, which was also unusual. He entered the shed to get the animals' food. But it was all gone. He was completely puzzled by what could have happened to it, or, for that matter, by everything that he had already witnessed this morning. He walked past the pond and he discovered that the fish had gone. 'What happened out here during the night?' he thought.

He then went back inside the house. He lived alone, but, with the company of his animals, he never really felt alone. He decided he needed to have a drink before he went outside again. He thought about the previous night: he never heard anything unusual. It had been quiet around the farm during the night so something that could cause havoc during the night without a sound being heard was hard to explain.

He drank up his coffee quickly and got some food together for the pigs. He just threw together a bit of anything and everything. The last pieces of bread, some fruit and veg, some left over soup and gravy. When it was ready, he took it to the pigs. On the way there he stepped in something messy and slimy. 'Now what?' he thought looking at the awful state of the bottom of his not so long ago cleaned and polished boots. He dragged his feet along the ground to get the worst of it off and gave the pigs their food. They didn't seem to be very hungry and left half of their food. Frederson just tried to get the place cleared up and everything the way it should be. There was still the mystery of the missing fish and food. Also, where could that awful slime have come from?

The rest of the day was rather normal and typical of his daily work on the farm, which was a relief for Frederson. Maybe a wild animal of some kind came during the night and spooked the animals and ate the fish and food. He kept thinking all of these possibilities, but they didn't seem to make much sense to him.

Once he had a pretty good afternoon and evening he started to forget about the morning. He went indoors a bit earlier than normal to relax and take all his stress away, feet up with a hot drink and some dinner. After eating he fancied a bit of reading, so he finished the book he had been reading for the last few days about knights in battle. 'Wonderful story,' he said as he closed the book. Then he went to bed.

The next morning, he woke up and it was another perfectly sunny day and he slept rather well. He soon got dressed and headed downstairs to his kitchen and made his porridge and coffee. Once he stepped outside, he saw some white feathers on the ground and, as he picked them up, he thought they looked like chicken feathers. As he looked ahead, he saw some more, further down the path. He then headed over to the chickens' pen. It was a complete mess again, like yesterday, but now the chickens were nowhere to be seen. 'How could they get out with the door still locked?' Thought Frederson. Something was going on around here. He had no idea what, but he still knew that he didn't like it. All the fruit from his trees were gone. He was getting angry now. The fruit he grew on his farm went to the market traders. 'Jack won't be happy when he comes to collect his stock.'

Walterwitz was having a little browse through the market. He came up to a fruit stall that belonged to one of his friends, Jack. 'Morning, Walterwitz. I know you enjoy your apples, but I couldn't get any today. The farm has no stock at the moment. He couldn't even tell me when he would. That's unusual, because Frederson's stock is normally great, as he does such hard work and takes so much care with it all.'

Walterwitz seemed a little puzzled, then he said, 'Of course. He is a good working and honest fellow and I am sure he will have more soon. Maybe I should go see him, I'd be happy to help him if he would like me to.'

Poor Frederson didn't have any more apples and he was going mad. First the animal food and fruit had been taken, as well as his fish, but now his chickens had vanished and the rest of his animals were not acting like their normal selves at all. While he was thinking about where the chickens were, he went around the farm to check the wellbeing of the other animals. The pigs were most unhappy, as Frederson tried to give them some food but they wouldn't have any. They just ran around screaming. The horses were very spooked. Once he calmed them down as much as he could, they wouldn't eat or sleep for the rest of the day.

Walterwitz was walking along the pathway leading up to the farm. He heard a funny noise. He turned and saw a chicken in the overgrown grass. He moved along so he was near the gate, and then he saw Frederson approach it with a brown sack which he had left by the gate. Walterwitz couldn't help but notice that he seemed very concerned about something.

'Oh, hello there,' said Frederson.

'There's no smile on your face and you seem to be rather startled, are you feeling ok my friend?'

'I'm having a rather hard day, Walterwitz. The animals are very stressed about something and I seem to have lost some, and some other strange things have been going on.'

'I came to ask if you needed any help, and about what happened to your fruit.'

'I don't know what happened to it. I am sorry for that, but something is going on around here, I told you about the animals. But also, some food and other things have been stolen. I haven't heard or seen any thieves or dangerous creatures about. I came across some awful slime yesterday and I have no idea where it came from and my chickens have now disappeared even though the pens door is still closed up.'

'Oh, I just saw a chicken out here. It must be one of yours.'

They went down along the grass outside the farm slowly and quietly. Frederson soon saw the chicken and crouched down. He stayed still and silent to let the chicken get closer. He tried to peek through the long grass and saw that it was facing the opposite way, and he reached out with both arms and snatched it up.

'Good job,' said Walterwitz.

Frederson wasted no time in taking the chicken straight to the pen. 'Well, that's one. Did you see another two anywhere?'

'No, I didn't, but I shall help you get them back.'

Walterwitz and Frederson searched the overgrown fields all around the farm. Eventually they were found, but how they got out remained a mystery. Even Walterwitz could not think of anything that would explain it. Frederson was happy to have found the chickens and to have them returned safely, but he was still rather worried about everything that had happened on the farm.

What happened to the apples was also on their minds. Frederson went around checking the rest of his livestock, although a lot of it was missing. His runner beans were still in place, although they had been fiddled with.

'There must be a thief about somewhere,' said Walterwitz. 'For now, let's go inside and have some nice tea. Now we have chickens back, it should help you relax a little.'

They did just that. As Walterwitz took a seat at the kitchen table, Frederson made a pot of tea and got the biscuits out. It was a nice break for Frederson as they sat down and had a nice chat while having some biscuits then Frederson poured out their tea. They were two of the few things that were still just as good and unspoiled as ever.

'The day when there is no good tea to drink is when we all will truly be in trouble,' said Walterwitz.

Frederson smiled and nodded. 'That is why you're the wizard my friend, always very cool and wise.'

Frederson drank up the last mouthful of his tea and placed his cup down. 'We should have some cake next time we spend some peaceful time together. That is always a thing to do when enjoying old classic tea. It is very enjoyable and relaxing to make, too, and I have recently filled some new recipes.'

Walterwitz seemed to be thinking for a quick moment. 'Well, I don't eat cake normally, but I guess just a little bit now and then won't hurt, and you are known for your good food.'

There were noises coming from outside, like heavy thumping sounds. Walterwitz went for a walk around the area. He was walking through the long grass, when he stepped in some piece of meat. He found that rather interesting and carefully looked around to see if he could spot another clue. He couldn't see anything just then, so he walked on. He reached the end of the area and was now going over hills. He then saw, just out of the corner of his eye, that there was a big hole in the side of one. He slowly walked over to take a look. He could hear snoring from inside. He gently lit the end of his staff, and then he saw some figure on the floor. It was a small and ugly looking thing. He recognised it — it was the troll his father had put a spell on when he was a child.

In the middle of this hole, he tried not to make a noise, but it was too late and the troll woke up. 'What are you doing? Go away! I will crush every bone in your body and make you my stew for lunch!'

Walterwitz knew the troublesome troll had to be responsible for all the unpleasant things going on at Greenwood farm. He simply fired his staff at the troll's head, making him scream in anger.

'Ouch!' The troll then stood up. 'You! You damn wizards will rue the day you crossed me.'

'I think we have had enough of your trouble!'

'Curse you, you old fool!'

'You have no power to curse anyone, you little slime ball. I think my father made a fine example of that. I shall now finish off what he started.'

Walterwitz held out his staff, and then several bolts of lightning came shooting out filling the room. 'Get away from here! If you ever go near the farm or city again, I shall turn you to dust!'

The room was filled by thunder. The troll screamed and

ran out and through the field. He was never seen again.

Walterwitz headed back to the farm. He told him that he shouldn't have any more trouble, for he just chased off a vile little thief. He spent the evening with Frederson. He ended up falling asleep in his big comfy chair. When he woke up it was time to go. Once he left the farm, he saw, across the field, some large figure hanging around.

'Not another troll! A full size one too!'

He walked over to it, keeping a sharp eye. As he got closer the figure was standing still. He could see its face, and it was certainly a troll. But there seemed to be something different about it. It didn't have the kind of expression or behaviour of any other troll he had come across.

'I'm Walterwitz, the local wizard. I help the people of the city when needed and wanted. Who are you and what do you want?'

'I am Eglog. I am looking for a place to stay that's safe and can provide me food. My homeland was taken from me when I was small.'

'I'm sorry to hear that, fellow. But I don't think there are many or any places that are much good for a troll in these parts. I know there was a cave that trolls used a long time ago. But other animals and nature have taken over it. We haven't seen any trolls around for a long time.'

'Most of them were killed by the giants. They took my land and ate everything. I had no choice but to leave and find somewhere else.'

'Giants? I thought they all died a very long time ago. Maybe I can help you out with that, fellow.'

They headed back to the farm. They decided to set off

in the morning. Walterwitz quickly got some food from his castle for Eglog to have. Frederson let Eglog sleep in his straw-filled barn. The next morning, Walterwitz was out first thing to get meat from town for Eglog. He was ready for the long journey back home. They walked back across the land that Eglog had come along. They told each other stories of their past. Now that Eglog had someone to talk to and had had a good night's rest, as well as food, he was feeling a lot better. The journey back to the home land didn't seem as long this time. Through large fields and woods, they went, just before the mountains were visible.

Eglog hadn't been to his family home mountains since he was little and with his parents. But he was still able to recognise the land, all the same. Among the mountains there was a smoking volcano. They had come all this way — they could not just turn back now. They would simply continue, but they would try to be prepared for anything that should happen.

'I don't remember anything about there being a volcano.'

'Sometimes a mountain is really a volcano, and nobody knows it.'

He could see eagles about. It started with just a few. Then he went on. He kept seeing more. At least they were still around. But if the giants weren't able to catch them, he didn't like his chances of doing it. He carried on going.

'Maybe we're getting close to the eagle's home.' They started to see more mountains. They carried on, taking in the new hostile and unfamiliar land. There were large torches on the mountainside. They seemed to have arrived at the mountains of the giants. They walked along as they saw more mountains. The mountains now had large gaps in them — it looked like they were doorways. There were no sights or sounds of giants yet. But there was a rumbling noise. It seemed to be from the mountains. It's unlikely to be from the sky on a clear day like this.

'The rumble of a miserable beast,' Eglog said.

They started to head towards one of the gapped mountains. Making sure there was nothing around. Then he saw a big ugly mug show its face from the dark shadows, and then soon went back inside. Then the back of another giant appeared from a mountain and went in the same way that the other giant's head had gone. There was an awful noise of muttering.

Walterwitz crouched behind a rock to have a think. Eglog had now gotten closer to the cave. He then took a rest on the side of a mountain. Then, peaking over the rock, he saw the two giants come out of the mountain, and then disappeared in to another. He went around the mountain and headed for the mountain that the giants had left. He checked the cave where the giants went, and it seemed all clear. Inside the cave he could see inscriptions on the way, in the traditional language of the giants, he assumed. There was a glow ahead. He thought it was probably a torch on the wall. He crept forward, careful not to be heard or seen. Although, if he were to be seen now, there was nowhere to hide. He went around a corner, and he could see a young-looking giant asleep. There was a large plate on the ground next to the sleeping giant. It was full of meat. Without hesitation, Eglog crept over to get what he could. He wasn't sure what meat it was, but he didn't want to think about it much. He just ate, or chewed it as fast as he could. It was an awkward place to be. Either the giant could wake up, or another could appear. But he thought he would hear a giant approaching first if it came along.

He then saw a shiny object in a corner. He went to pick it up. Then the young giant started to wake up. Eglog still had the object in his hand, but without a thought he just ran out with it in his hand. He ran out the cave, and then he must have been seen, or detected, as a load of loud bellowing and noises from the giants began. He went around some rock and hid there. He then noticed that what he had seen in the cave was still in his hand. It was a crest with another inscription. He just dropped it and moved on. He heard a load of heavy footsteps all around him. The moans and groans of giants were getting louder. He wondered where Walterwitz had gone. But he didn't dare call out or look around for him. He saw another doorway in a mountain. This was one of the smaller ones, and he could see most of the inside as it was in direct sunlight. He went inside to hide and shelter. A giant saw him go in there, so it sat with its back against the hole trapping Eglog inside.

Walterwitz was moving around trying to see where Eglog had gone to. He walked along and saw a giant was standing behind the mountain in front of him. He quickly hid behind a rock. He wanted to find Eglog before he tried to make a plan concerning the giants. But then it sounded like the giant was coming. Then he heard a rubble noise nearby, and saw the rocks nearby move until a man's face suddenly appeared.

'Down here,' he said to Walterwitz while holding the rock above his head. Walterwitz was not really sure if he should, but the giants were about. So, without too much thought, he quickly went down with the little fellow. It was quite a squeeze for him as he went down through the gap, but he managed to get through.

He found himself in an underground cave, with a dwarf there. 'Hello. I'm Bimmy. We are safe down here. At least, we always have been to date'.

Walterwitz looked around and down the cave. Then he looked at Bimmy. 'What is this place?'

'It's our home. The dwarf race has lived here, deep under the mountains, for many years. Let's go down the stairway to the main cave town.'

Down they went, through this small passage. They got to the top of the stairs. It was a long way down to the bottom. Walterwitz looked in awe at the town. There were countless huts. Each one had brightly lit torches on their front porches. There were three large towers, the top of each one was topped by a torch. High up, Walterwitz could see a hole in the top of the mountain where the smoke went through.

'I thought this was a volcano when I was outside.'

They reached the bottom of the steps, finally. Walterwitz soon became the centre of attention, and everybody was staring at him. Some gave him a dirty look, others looked at him curiously. There were many dwarfs about. Walterwitz wondered where they all came from and how they could all live down there underground, although their town was impressive. They walked down a path, and Bimmy stopped outside a bar.

'My team are inside, come meet them before we continue.'

They went inside the bar. The closest table to the door was

round and had dwarfs sitting around it. 'Fellows,' said Bimmy. 'I introduce you to Walterwitz here, from the land above. He has been in the giants' land, and lived to tell about it. Walterwitz, I introduce you to Blammy and Blanter, the masters of beer drinking, and Tamon and Tankard, the masters of gambling.'

'There is a cabin just over here, where you can stay for a while. You will be safe down here with us.'

Walterwitz was shown to his cabin. He still had the crest in his hand, so he placed it down on a small round table.

Bimmy looked at it with wide eyes. 'Where did you get that?'

'Up on the ground, just before you called me.'

'It looks like a crest of the dwarf lords, for whom the mountains were home before the giants took over. Our leader should have it. He will be very interested, I'm sure.'

'I was told that trolls lived in these parts before giants took over.'

'Trolls did live up there. But who they were really for, is perhaps another story.'

'Who is this leader that you speak?'

'His name is Bones Mcgollen, he is our wisest veteran. He is the only one to remember the lives of dwarfs in the mountains. The crest has a place over his fire place.'

'I will be happy to return it to him.'

'I'm sure he would appreciate it. He may like to return the favour.' They set off to the home of Bones Mcgollen. Bimmy knocked on the front door, but there was no reply. Walterwitz thought no one was there, but Bimmy kept waiting. Then the door slowly opened.

'Mr Mcgollen, nice to see you. We have something for you.' Bimmy then looked at Walterwitz's hand.

He held out his hand with the crest and the old dwarf looked at it, and then cupped it in his hand. He didn't say anything, but his gratitude was clear. He gestured for them to enter his home. They stepped in and Bones walked over to his fireplace and slid the crest in its place. Then there was a soft click. The fireplace then opened up, and a passageway was there.

Bimmy crouched and went through. He went into a room, but he needed light. Walterwitz fetched a torch, then Bimmy could see in the room. On the walls were more of the inscriptions, all around the room. In the middle of the room was a well. The well also had the inscriptions around it. It was full of water. But when he dipped his finger in it, it didn't seem like water. It was so thick. It wouldn't splash or ripple.

He then went back to Bones and Walterwitz. 'There is a well in there. There is water in it. Only, it's not like actual water. It's more like a solid. The marking on the crest is all around the room and the well.'

Bones thought it sounded familiar. 'Sounds like that could be the well of will. I heard about it. It's supposed to lead to the river of Miver. Miver was, according to legend, a spirit in the river that would use its power to assist those in need.'

'I, too, have heard of Miver. She knew my father, I believe,' Walterwitz said. 'I would be interested in seeing her and hearing what she would have to say myself.'

'Why have you come here? What do you truly seek?' asked Bones.

'I met a surviving troll, far away from here. He told me how this was his home until the giants took it.'

'So, you're going to get his home back.'

'I told him I would. I never met a troll with his temperament. This is where he is from. I don't think he would blend in with the city very well. He would probably need as much food as everyone else added together.'

'I don't know if there's anything left here for eating anyway.'

'The giants are still here. What do they eat?'

'I am not sure. Do giants and trolls eat the same things?'

'I don't see why not. Until today I had never actually seen one. I certainly haven't seen them eat.'

'Where is this troll?'

'I lost him around the mountains. The giants were about. I really should soon get going, he could be in danger.'

'Maybe Miver could help him, or tell you where he is.'

Walterwitz headed through the fireplace to have a look at the well. He saw that it was exactly like Bimmy said. The inscriptions that were in the area also had him thinking. Maybe the trolls had put them about. Or maybe they date back even further than them. Could there be something important in the writing that could help defend the land from the giants? Looking in the well, he wondered what was really at the other end. He eventually just got up on the well and jumped.

He landed on solid ground — next to him was a river. He looked around him, further along the river to his right there was light and the end of the tunnel. Nobody was around that he could see or hear. He somehow knew of a presence there with him. He just felt that the eyes and mind of somebody was on him. His mind was also on theirs.

After standing around in silence he decided to just get on with it. If this Miver was down there like he thought, she would help. 'I'm sure you know who I am and that I am here to see if you can tell me what I need to know.'

'Yes. You help the less fortunate. You have enough power yourself to defeat the foes of your friends. One of them is in a cave, trapped by a giant. They will probably soon kill him and then eat him if help doesn't come to him soon enough.'

A boat suddenly appeared in front of Walterwitz. 'Go down river to the outside. Go up the hillside and then you shall see the giant that has him trapped. Be quick and you can do it before the other giants come over to him.'

Walterwitz quickly stepped into the boat and rowed down to the end of the tunnel. He was soon there, after his good rowing. Miver may have also blown the flow of the river. Once he reached the tunnel's end, he pulled the boat over to the side and climbed out. It was a pretty steep climb up and it went a rather long way. Once he reached the top, with the giant's head in sight, he was out of breath.

He held up his staff so it shined brightly in the giant's eyes. It helped give Walterwitz a moment to get his breath while the giants attention was now on him.

'You little wrench! I crush your bones!'

Now he was getting his breath back — he got out his sword as the giant stomped over to him. It tried to quickly grab Walterwitz, but he sliced him with his hand. Eglog came out of the cave and saw Walterwitz. Walterwitz used the staff to attack the giants. Eglog wanted to use the sword when he saw Walterwitz hold it up.

'Let me have it!' Eglog shouted out.

The sword was thrown towards Eglog. Walterwitz used the power of the staff to keep the giant away from him and to weaken the giant. When the giant was looking away from him, Eglog held up the sword with both arms and drove it into the giant. It then stumbled to one knee. Eglog pulled out the sword — and then drove it into the giant's skull.

The giant was dead.

The others would surely come for revenge and self-defence. They moved away as quickly as they could, and there were no signs of any giants. They went back to the cave Eglog had hidden in.

'I found some people and fascinating places around here.' Walterwitz then told Eglog about the dwarf who led him to their underground civilization, the well and river and how he knew where to find Eglog.

Eglog found it interesting, but some of it was a bit hard for him to believe. 'Well, I guess we could do with all the help we can get. If we all work together then we can make things better for everyone.'

It was now rather quiet about. They thought that the giants would have heard the shouts and noises from their fight with the first giant. They started to walk around, out of the cave and over to where the giants may be. Walterwitz had his staff and Eglog kept the sword. He had shown he had quite a skill and ease with it. They then entered the cave of a mountain. It sounded like there was snoring inside.

Walterwitz began to think about an attempt to talk with the giant. Maybe he could learn from him about where they all came from and if they could perhaps find a way to be a bit civil with other races. Or the civilizations of humans and wizards would be the next ones destroyed. Eglog, on the other hand, only thought about killing the giant.

'Let's just get them all before they get us. I don't think they will ever like us now that we have killed one of them.'

'But we need to be careful. We don't know how many there are, or how much they're capable of. If we are faced with two or three at once, we might be in big trouble.'

'You were told that you could stop them. I am here with you too.'

Eglog quickly drove the sword into the giant's skull. It was rather tough, as their skulls are thick and tough, but the giant was dead all right. Stepping around the mountains, a couple more giants were about and spotted them, and then went for them. Walterwitz and Eglog were ready and waiting for them. Then suddenly the dwarfs appeared. Bimmy, Blammy and Blanter, came from one side and attacked the giants' feet with their axes. Tamon and Tankard came from the other side, throwing knives at the giants. With Walterwitz also attacking them with his magical staff, the giants were falling down. Eglog had waited a long time for this moment and did not waste it — he soon struck the sword into the closest giant's heart. The other giants managed to get back on their feet, and throw rocks towards Walterwitz, and kick a wave of dirt and dust at the dwarfs.

They went away in fury and stomped across the land and eventually disappeared over the horizon.

'What if they come back, and bring more with them?' asked Eglog.

'Then you could all just fight them off just as fine as you just did,' Walterwitz said. He looked over to where the giants went. 'They may just find some other place to say.

Far away is the land they are meant to have come from. They should just stay there, unless something drove them away from there too.' He looked at the dwarfs. 'You also have these good men nearby. I am sure they will make fine neighbours.'

Eglog then went to slice the leg off the giant in the cave. 'All these events have made me rather hungry.'

Walterwitz waved goodbye to Eglog as he went off. Then he walked along with the dwarfs. 'I think I shall stay in the room Mr Mcgollen offered me to sleep in, before heading home. Before tonight is over, I shall join you for the biggest night of gambling and drinking you've ever had.'

ALLYANA

It was a lovely sunny day, so Walterwitz went to the park. It was a very nice and relaxing park with birds singing in the trees, people with their dogs, children playing, and a wonderful wildlife pond. As Walterwitz entered the park, a little Jack Russel came over, barking in excitement and wagging its little tail. Walterwitz said hello to the dog and patted its head. He was always very fond of dogs, and they liked him too. He took a seat on the park bench, and took a deep breath to relax. He wanted to enjoy the moment before something terrible came up. Like, having to face an evil villain or beast, sort out the mess that some damn fool had gotten himself into, assist the king in all his vanity, or go back to his castle, which needed a lot of cleaning done.

He closed his eyes with the sun and soft breeze in his face and listened to the birds singing. 'Walterwitz! Walterwitz!' shouted some children who were running over to him.

'Oh, damn it,' went Walterwitz as he opened his eyes.

The children stopped by his feet. 'What did you say?'

'Oh, dommits. It's a wizard's word.' He grinned while lying to the children, with their innocent big eyes staring at him. 'What can I do for you, lovely little angels?'

'Can you do a magic trick? Or a few?'

'Sorry, but I left my magic wand at home.'

'Oh no,' they said, just before walking away.

Of course Walterwitz could still perform certain tricks without his wand, but the kids didn't know that. Sometimes an old wizard just needs his time and space to think about time and space. He didn't have that much time to relax and he would be going to the astronomy club that evening.

As the children walked away, they started playing again, but now they were closer to Walterwitz than before, which the wizard didn't quite appreciate. He tried to ignore them and just listen to the birds, but he couldn't hear them. The children must have scared them away. But Walterwitz did his best to stay calm and polite. More than ever, when it was the children.

'Oh, dear sweet little halflings,' he called out. 'Please try not to make too much noise for us silly old fools who need peace.'

The children then went over to Walterwitz with pity. 'Oh, you're not a silly old fool, you're great,' they said as Walterwitz sighed as that backfired on him.

'Yes, well, thank you very much, children. Now run along, I need some thinking time.' He then noticed that Charlie was sitting alone by the pond. 'Why don't you go and see Charlie over there?'

'We have enough of us already, and he doesn't normally want to play with us. Maybe you should ask him why.'

'Oh, what the heck,' thought Walterwitz, as he got up and headed over to where Charlie was sitting. He wasn't going to get his peace anyway. 'Charlie, dear boy, what are you doing over here?'

'I'm bored. I never go anywhere or do anything exciting. My parents can't afford anything and they always have to work. So I just come here and watch the fish swim.

I find it very nice.'

'Yes, so do I,' replied Walterwitz as they then just watched the fish, frogs, and dragonflies living in harmony. After a while, Walterwitz looked back to the rest of the park, and saw that the other children had gone. There was just a woman with a dog, who was now heading out of the park.

Charlie then went on, 'I've always wanted to go to the sea and swim with the animals there, but I've never seen the sea.'

'I see. Well, we are right here with some lovely little animals in this lovely area of wildlife. We can only see those that come up near the surface. As well as those that can go on the dry part. Like when the frogs come up onto the rocks, and the little insects come up on the lily pads and flowers. The pond is rather deep, it would be nice to see what's at the bottom, don't you think so?'

'Yes, I do. There are probably lots of fish down there.'

'Yes, I'm sure there are, boyo.' As Walterwitz said that he pulled out his sword and held it in his hand with his staff in the other. Holding the two, a bright light appeared as he started mumbling to himself. Charlie couldn't understand a thing. As the light, within a few seconds, got huge, it went all over Charlie, so that he couldn't see anything. He felt very strange and had a tingly feeling all over his body.

The light cleared up and Walterwitz was standing there with him. Charlie looked at the pond. It seemed to be huge. He thought about how that could have happened, and then he looked at the park, which also looked much bigger. Walterwitz had shrunk them down to tiny size. If they hadn't also shrunk, they would fit perfectly in one of their pockets. Charlie felt many different things. He was happy, nervous, amazed, adventurous, and he didn't know what to do or say. Walterwitz then looked at him, trying not to grin.

'Are you okay?'

'Yes, I think so. But this is very strange. What are we doing?'

'Well, it would be nice to go see all the wildlife up close and personal, for both you and me. So let's go, before a dog comes along and eats us.' Walterwitz then grabbed a hold of Charlies hand and they jumped into the pond.

Once the water around them cleared up, they could see Shubunkin fish coming over towards them. Walterwitz and Charlie stayed where they were as the fish gracefully swam past. Then, slowly and carefully they swam forward to where they saw more fish swimming about. They started to swim towards the fish, but then they suddenly shot off in all different directions. Walterwitz kept hold of Charlie as the fish darted by, trying to avoid the two of them being hit. They could then see a giant bird beak dipping in and out of the water. Walterwitz, while holding Charlie, swam down south towards the middle of the water out of the birds reach.

In this area it was just a big clearing with nothing to see, so they swam down some more. They could now see some big leaves and grass, with lots of fish around and they quickly went down towards them. They reached the ground, where there were Tench and Minnows. Charlie was amazed to see the fish so close and big to him, he saw details on them that he never knew about before. Then a couple of worms swam right by, which he didn't like. There were many other bugs about, too, which he would shoo away. After a few more minutes of all these bugs annoying him, he would soon start to have enough.

Walterwitz then saw something large moving in the distance, so they slowly swam by the fish. They were now closer — there were two sturgeons by a load of rocks. Something was wandering about in front of them. The sturgeons looked vicious and they seemed to be snapping their teeth at the nearby creatures. Then, Walterwitz caught a glimpse of what looked like a human face on the creature near the rocks. It was hard to see clearly through the pond water, but there was a strange feeling about it. He thought he shouldn't get any closer than he already was while he had Charlie with him and they were that size. He could put Charlie in terrible danger.

Walterwitz then turned arounds and headed back to where they had come from and they started to swim back up towards the surface. They went up to where the rocks are and leaned on them while they caught their breath and had a little rest. Walterwitz climbed up on the rock, and then a Goldfish started having a nibble at Charlie's feet.

'Ahh!' he went.

Walterwitz quickly grabbed his arms and pulled him out. Then a bird landed on one of the rocks. Looking at the two of them, it hopped onto a closer rock. That was enough for Walterwitz — he zapped it with his staff. He and Charlie then jumped along on to each rock and onto the grass. The grass was rather long, so it was rather hard to walk through. Once they were far enough away from the pond, Walterwitz tried to see and hear anyone in the park, but that was also hard for him to do. He then just held up his sword, which beamed in the sunlight, and started mumbling again. As there was a big, bright, white flash, Walterwitz and Charlie were back to full, normal size.

'I think that's enough for today, Mister Charli. Maybe we shall have some more exciting adventures some other time.'

'Okay, it would be nice to do it again sometime.'

'Yes, but for now you might be better off at home, where you are safe, and with your parents.' Walterwitz then walked with Charlie as he went home.

Once having seen Charlie to his home, Walterwitz went back to the park. He sat on the bench enjoyed the moment of peace with the whole park to himself. He listened for the birds, but there was none around. He then took a look at the pond. He then remembered seeing something strange down there, like a person. 'How could that be?' he thought.

He soon got up and walked over to the pond. It all looked normal, but when he thought about what he saw earlier, down there, it gave him a terrible feeling. He crouched down to take a closer look through the water. He had quite the urge to see what was going on down by those rocks. He then took a quick look around him. There was nobody around and he shrunk himself back to tiny size.

He then dove into the pond, and swam down towards the bottom. He had to stop to swim around some of the fish, as he felt it would better to not get too close to them. As he started to reach the lower region of the pond, he slowed slightly, trying to have a good look without being seen. The big sturgeons were there, he could see. They were still around the pile of rocks. He was now getting very close to the ground and he couldn't see any sign of the figure he had seen before.

He landed down on the clearing in front of the rocks. The sturgeons were glaring at him. He knew it would be silly to just walk forwards, as they certainly looked territorial. He turned around and a man, wearing a black robe, was standing right there in front of him. He was pretty sure that this was the person he was looking for.

'Who are you and what are you doing here?'

'Why? What's going on down here? Who are you?'

'I am Kiddal, my wife, Allyana of Aqua ground is being held captive in there. Are you one of them?'

'No. I am Walterwitz. I wanted to get a closer look at things down here. Your wife is held captive?'

'Yes, in there. It's that wicked wizard of the wild waters.'

Walterwitz had a rather blank stare on his face for a few seconds. 'What in the wisest wizard's world is that?'

'The wizard that rules these parts. Shouldn't you know about other wizards? Or are you not a very good wizard?'

'I know other wizards, but I've never heard of this kind before.'

'You are not from this area, are you?'

'Well in a way, yes, I'm usually up on land, but maybe I can help.'

'I don't know, maybe you can, if you know how to handle this kind of dangerous situation.'

'Well, there is nothing wrong with giving it a try.'

Walterwitz then approached the two large sturgeons, looking down on him. 'You in there! Come out and show yourself! Explain yourself to me and show your worth!'

Kiddal, suddenly feeling more confident with himself went to Walterwitz's side and also called out to the wizard. 'Yeah, come on out and face your enemy like a man.'

But there was no response. Walterwitz took a few steps

forward, keeping a sharp eye on those deadly fish.

'Hand the lady over to me,' Kiddal went. 'Anything happens to her and you will answer to me! Foolish scum!'

Then one of the rocks moved slightly, leaving a gap. A large tentacle came out, grabbed Kiddal, lifted him off his feet, and pulled him straight back into the cave. With Kiddal yelling all the way, he went straight inside the rocks and the gap closed behind. It all left Walterwitz rather stumped.

He then turned his attention back to the two large fish. He pulled out his sword and held it out in front of him. It probably wasn't enough to make the beasts feel very threatened, but they never took their eyes off him as he slowly walked closer to them. He then fired a bolt of lightning from the sword into the face of the closest fish. It worked, but his powers were weaker underwater. The fish was rather angry. It got closer to him. He kept an eye on it, it, then stopped. It let the other fish do the work, as Walterwitz held his sword up. This time he fired several bolts of lightning at the fish, which stunned it.

Walterwitz tried to strike him with the sword, but the other sturgeon was charging at him. He backed away as the stunned fish started to approach. It got in the other sturgeon's way and smacked into the back of its head. This made it angry and took a bite at the other fish. Walterwitz wasted no time, and when the sturgeon was facing away from him, he took a great big swing with his sword and sliced the beast's head off.

The other fish was eyeing up Walterwitz, moving from left to right. Walterwitz would fire some bolts of lightning, but they all missed as the fish was ready for whatever he would dish out. He then swam around the rock pile, out of sight, and carried on going around to the other side. Just before the sturgeon was able to turn around, having realised the wizard was behind him, Walterwitz fired several bolts. The big fish was stunned but angry.

Walterwitz stepped closer to swing his sword. He swung it at the beast as hard as he could underwater. The beast reacted and caught the sword between its teeth. Walterwitz fired more lightning through the sword, making the fish stumble. He now decided he had had enough and swam off.

Walterwitz tried to relax as he watched it swim away. He then walked towards the rocks and had a good look and feel. Then the big tentacle came out and grabbed Walterwitz tight and pulled him inside. He could see Kiddal and a woman who must have been Allyana, in a cage. The tentacle was that of a big octopus that was sitting on the ceiling. It shook Walterwitz abo. He struck with the sword through its tentacle. It then spat toxins at Walterwitz, but they missed him. Then the octopus climbed down the wall. It struck at Walterwitz with its tentacles, but he ducked to avoid them. The octopus then went straight over to Walterwitz for a close-up attack. Walterwitz struck the sword right into the head of the octopus.

He then went over to the cage of Allyana and Kiddal, checking that they were ok, and to see how to open it. There was a small keyhole, but there was no key about or anything else that could be used.

'Why don't you use your magic to get us out?' asked Kiddal.

'I don't seem to be able to use much down here. I was able to use it outside, but I think that blew it.'

'I guess you're not such a great wizard after all then. The old wizard of the water uses lots of his magical powers here. I guess only he can get us out. We're doomed.'

'Be quiet, man. I will get you out, and deal with this wicked water wizard that you speak of. Any idea where he could be?'

Allyana and Kiddal both shook their heads.

Walterwitz headed out of the rock house to find the wizard. But before he did anything else, he swam up towards the surface, where he could rest on a rock for a moment. Quickly as possible, and without being seen by anyone or anything, he then headed back down to the bottom. He swam by the fish and around the pond to see what he could find, but there was no sign of the wizard. He was going around in circles, where nothing was new or different.

He stopped to have a think. He thought of another talk with Kiddal and Allyana, and then in the distance he saw something that immediately caught his eye. He swam over to what looked like a circle of water, like a portal to another world. He looked around, thinking if it was a trick or a trap. But he then decided to get closer and put his arm through. Everything became a blur.

Next thing he knew, he was standing in the water still, but it all seemed different. There was a large, unusual-looking plant in front of him. As he looked around, he saw that the fish looked different. There were large fish with multi-coloured, flowing fins. There were thousands of tiny red fish, and some eels swimming about. He then saw a lot of mounds in the distance.

He headed over towards them — they seemed to have

little doors on them. He saw a small person go by and carried on walking. Then he saw another man standing on the corner of a mound. He had a puzzled look on his face.

'Hello there, do you need some help?'

Walterwitz wasn't too sure what to say. 'I'm not really sure where I am. Or what this place is.'

'Oh dear, you are not local. Yes, that I could already tell. You look very strange.'

Then another person came up from behind the man, it seemed to be a woman with its slimmer body and long bright hair. 'This poor old man doesn't know where he is.'

'Is he a right-minded fellow? Look at his clothes and face. I've never seen anyone like it. Does he even know who he is?'

'My name is Walterwitz, and I come from the dry land. But while I was swimming in water I went through a strange portal and ended up here. I was looking for a wizard.'

'The wizard! Not that wizard?'

'I don't know what you mean.'

'There is only one wizard that we know of here. We try not to talk of him.'

'I need to find this wizard. Do you know where I can do that?'

'He has a hideout somewhere around here. We don't know where.'

Then the woman went, 'We are all having dinner in the community hall in a little while. Everyone will be there, maybe they could help. Have you eaten?'

'No.'

'Well, I'm sure you will be welcome. Our leaders should make you feel welcome.'

'Okay then, as long as it doesn't take too long. It would be nice.'

'I am Jolene, and this is Poisem.' Jolene then pointed in the direction Walterwitz was facing. 'Right to the end is the hall. Help yourself.'

Jolene and Poisem then went into their little house, leaving Walterwitz to wander down the road. He headed off down the road towards the large building, as he could see that it's large double doors were open. He got closer, and could see a man standing in the door way. The man gestured to Walterwitz to invite him inside. Inside the building was a load of large round dinner tables. Some were empty and some had people sitting, waiting and chatting.

Once Walterwitz had entered the room, a lot of the talking had stopped, and eyes turned to Walterwitz. Most of these people were dressed in simple white shirts, with cleanly shaved faces and their hair was short and tidy. He sat quietly at the nearby table, trying not to bring too much attention to himself. Then waiters came out and placed a load of plates and bowels of food around the tables.

There was a long table along the back of the room, which must have been for the people's leaders. Three men and two women came through a doorway and sat at the long table. Walterwitz started eating from the bowl on his table, which was labelled "Octopus soup". Before taking his seat, the man at the middle of the back table stood in front of his chair, looking around the room.

'Hello everybody and welcome.' He was met with applause. 'It is always a pleasure to see you all at our gathering.' He then looked at Walterwitz. 'It is also nice to see some new faces here. If you enjoy yourself, then please do tell friends and family about it.'

Walterwitz started to take a few sips of his soup. It wasn't really bad for his taste, but he wasn't hugely keen on it either. He took a taste of the drink that had been left on his table. He had never tasted anything like it before, and a strange fuzzy feeling went to his head. He was tempted to drink the rest of it, although his brain warned him against it. He took a couple of sips, more slowly this time. Then he tried more soup. It tasted really plain this time. He tried hard to finish it up, and the drink helped. He would take a sip of soup followed by the drink. He soon ran out of the drink and had the rest of the soup on its own. He soon called out to the waiter asking for another drink.

While finishing, he looked around the room. Everyone was just eating quietly. Some had the soup, and some seemed to have some large meaty meals. The waiter came with another glass for Walterwitz to drink. He was rather keen to get the taste out of his mouth. He also had the urge to taste the drink more. It was strange, and he wasn't even sure if he really liked it or not, but still found it very drinkable and he soon drank the entire glass. Maybe a bit too fast, as his head started to pound him. Walterwitz had had enough and wanted to get out of there and on with his duty. He then stood up, but it gave him a head rush. It was bad enough that the drink had got to him. He tried keeping cool and calm as he took a breath, but he just fainted.

When he woke up, he found himself lying on a sofa. One of the waiters was sitting on a chair, keeping an eye on him. 'Hello there, fella, how are you?'

'Oh, I guess I feel fine now, thank you. I'm not sure what happened now. My head just went mad all over.'

'Well, you seemed to have had a bit to drink. Try and be more careful in future.' The waiter then stood up and went through the doorway, 'I shall tell the governor that you are awake.'

Walterwitz then tried to stand up, and he did it fine. His head felt normal, apart from feeling a bit of shame. Then the man who had spoken at the head table came in, with a charming smile.

'Hello there, sir, I'm glad to see you are well. That was quite a scare for us out there. We used to get a rather regular number of fainter-drinkers, but we seemed to have got out of that habit.'

'Well, what is that you drink here anyway?'

'Oh, it's a traditional cocktail that our ancestors left us. It was said to have been created by accident, during the search for a magic potion by mixing liquids and other natural resources. They never did get that, though.'

'That is interesting, but I can't stay any longer. I'm trying to track down somebody known as the wizard of the wild waters, if you could help.'

There was a little pause where the governor said and did nothing. 'I believe he lives away beyond the other side of town in some hut. I wouldn't recommend going to see him.'

'I know how to handle troublesome folk like him. I need to help someone, and I need to bring this wizard to justice.'

'Well, okay then, if you are sure you are feeling up to it. Your head should clear up by the time you get there. If it hasn't already, that is, but you do seem fine.'

'Yes, indeed. So, on the other side of town in a hut, is

it?'

'Yes, but it is quite a walk. Once you've left town, you will have to go through a rather barren and unpleasant land.' The governor then walked the two of them out of the room, through to the front doors — some people were still in the hall as they went through.

'Well, go to the end down that way, then turn left and then straight ahead. That will take you out of town, but beyond that I can't really give directions. If you would like, I can ask someone to assist you.'

'Thank you, but I'm okay. I will find my way, if it's the last thing I do.'

'Well, you do seem driven in your task, good luck to you.'

As the wizard headed down the road in the direction he was given, he marvelled at the sights around him. It was a moment that Walterwitz couldn't help but feel a bit excited by, as it was a whole different world to explore. But he walked down the road and then turned left as the governor directed. There was nothing to see, just more mounds with a door at the front. There was no sign of any people around and all was quiet. Looking as far as he could the land truly did become barren and featureless. 'Should be easy enough to spot a cave here,' Walterwitz thought.

He carried on looking for anything that stood out or looked interesting. He saw nothing for some time. It even got to the point that when he looked behind it was all just barren.

He had to be careful, and thought that he should probably keep going in a straight line. At least he knew where to go to get back to where he started. But, to have a proper search of the area, he would have to move in a different direction.

Then he thought he saw movement beneath the sand, maybe it was his mind playing games. But he then saw something else shift through the sand, and he could have sworn that he saw a pair of eyes too. He looked ahead and saw it again, and tried to follow it. He lost sight of it, but saw something else further ahead. He moved on. It looked like a shape in the distance. This had to be the hut of the wizard.

As he got closer, the hut, of course, became clearer. It seemed normal and innocent enough from outside, but some evil was alleged to live here. Walterwitz kept alert as he knocked on the door.

There was a whiney voice from inside. 'Who's there?'

'The wizard!'

The door was opened, and some short figure dressed in a black robe was there. 'You're not the wizard!'

'I am where I come from, and I dare say that I am here too.'

'Go away, you silly old git!' He tried shutting the door but Walterwitz put his foot in.

'The wizard will see to you.'

'I am a wizard. I shall see to you if you don't make yourself more pleasant and helpful. Tell me where this other wizard is, or I'll turn you into something even smaller and more disgusting than you already are.'

'You wouldn't dare harm me. You are probably a terrible wizard, if you are one.'

'Do not test me.' Walterwitz went with a different tone, holding up his staff, which sparked.

'The wizard is out. I don't know where.' The little fellow started to panic, and then he just passed out.

He will be fine, Walterwitz thought. Then, as he looked forward, he saw some shiny objects on the other side of the room. One of them was a key. It looked like it was the one that he needed. He took hold of it and put it in his pocket. Now he just had to find the way back to the pond.

He remembered that the hut was facing the town. So, if he just went straight ahead, he should get back to the town okay. With all the walking today, as well as battling creatures underwater, it was proving to be a rather tiresome day. He walked on, fast as he could, yet not so fast that it wore him out. He just hoped he could find a way back home. The sandy building started to appear — he made his way towards the big hall. He got there okay. The doors to the hall were now closed. Instead of checking if anyone was in there, he headed to the point from which he had entered the land through the portal.

After walking up and down some roads, he finally came across the big plant that he had seen when he first arrived. He had no trouble recognizing that, or the red fish around it. 'Where to find these portals, and how?' he thought. He didn't really know anything about them. He would be in trouble if he couldn't find a way back to his world.

He figured that the governor was probably the best one to speak about it to. All he could do was go to the hall and see if he was still there. He went down the road, getting some funny looks from passers-by. Walterwitz approached the large doors of the hall and realised that they weren't closed right up. He gently pushed it open and poked his head through. Luckily, the governor was there, even though almost everyone else was gone, with just two other men at a round table.

'Hello there. Been to the wizard? Nice to see you made it back.'

'Hello. I'm fine. But I do now have a problem with finding my way home.'

'Oh, well, we will be happy to help if we can.'

'It is rather hard to explain. I'm from a very different and faraway place.'

'Yes, I figured that much.' The governor said with a smile.

'Well, basically, I stumbled upon a wormhole, or portal. These things are like, a door-way to another world. Or a different area, I think.'

The governor looked at Walterwitz with a slight change in his expression. 'I'm not really sure what you mean, sir. Do you, fellers?' He asked the two other men at the table.

'I think I have heard of something like this before,' said the man with curly hair and scar on his cheek.

He then looked at the man sitting between him and the governor. 'You've been around a lot, been in battles and travelled. Didn't you witness something like that?'

This man had long straight hair and a very clear looking face. 'I think so, a long time ago, when these old villains were about. They used these portals to go into different boies of water. The portals just come and go when someone uses them. That's about all I know.'

'I'm the governor, why wasn't I told about this?'

'I don't know, sir, you were probably too busy or something.'

'Okay, well if that is really all you can tell me, then, I

say thank you and goodbye,' Walterwitz said as he headed outside.

He could hear the three men muttering amongst each other as he went out. Although, he had no idea where to go next. Luckily, he got a clue as he went down a road and heard a load of shouting behind some large plants.

'Evil witch man about!' Someone shouted.

'He's gone,' someone else said. 'He just disappeared.'

Walterwitz quickly searched the area. And just then, it was rather hard to see, but Walterwitz could see the portal amongst a bunch of large and strange plants. Where it led to, he wasn't too sure. Walterwitz just ran up and dived through it.

He found himself on the ground. He looked around him as he got up. He thought he was back. It did look like he was back in the pond. He saw all those fish that he and Charlie swam by. He could see the rock pile where Allyana and Kiddal were captive. He headed over and entered the pile. Or was it supposed to be a house? 'That's not important right now,' Walterwitz thought. They were still in the cage — but of course they would be.

'I have a key. After all this, I just hope it's the right one.'

He started to walk over to the cage. Then there was a big, bright flash, causing Walterwitz to put his hands in front of him and look away. When it was gone, and he looked forward, a man was standing there. Bald-headed, with a long moustache, wearing a blue robe with a sword in his hand.

'Ah, you stupid, old beard-man. You may not release the queen of all Aqua ground. I am now supreme ruler of all, and any pesky fools will be put to death.'

Walterwitz got out his sword and held it out, clashing

with the wicked wizard's sword. They both pushed forward with their swords, in a great test of strength and skill. Then they would both step back and strike at the other. They circled each other, looking for a weakness or distraction that could be used. Walterwitz started to gain the control. As they locked swords again, the wicked wizard of water held out his other hand and a rock came flying over. Walterwitz sensed it coming and ducked as late as possible, making the wicked one of the waters get struck by it and knocked to the ground.

'That wasn't so smart or supreme was it,' said Kiddal.

The wizard got up and held up his sword and fired a powerful blast at Kiddal knocking him down. Walterwitz reacted fast and struck the wizard's back, and he fell to the ground with the sword right through him.

Walterwitz then got out the key and opened the cage. Kiddal was still down. Allyana tried to sit him up, and shouted at him. He then woke up, rubbing his head. He was still rather grumpy, probably more so than ever. So they all concluded that he was fine.

'I thank you for our rescue, and ridding us all of him,' Allyana said to Walterwitz. 'I can reward you if you like.'

'Oh no, that won't be necessary. I would just like to go home, if everything is fine with you now.'

'Of course, sir, you deserve your rest. Feel free to drop by any time. We could take you out to a big gathering that we know, and have dinner.'

'I shall keep that in mind. Thank you and goodbye.'

Walterwitz then swam up to the surface and climbed up on a rock. A bird pounced and grabbed Walterwitz and flew up into the air. Walterwitz held out his sword. The bird felt something. Walterwitz grew out of control for the bird to handle, back to his full size, and then landed straight into the pond again.

He felt something under his leg and pulled it out. It was Allyana and Kiddal in the palm of his hand. 'Oh! I am sorry for dropping in like that.'

SMIGERTON

'Hello, there, you bunch of little old troublesome misfits! Come to visit me, have you, eh? Well, that's all fine and nice, but if you bring out the unpleasant side of me and make me angry, well, you will feel theses boots up your rug-rat backsides!' Smigerton said to the children. Then he picked up his drink and gulped some down. 'Now, the old wizard may have told you some tales about me hunting geese or rabbits. Make sure you don't get in my way, or you will feel tremendous pain! I will find you a pain in my backside too!'

Walterwitz then decided to take the children around the rest of the castle. They all went on the balcony, where there was a great view of the land for miles around. They passed the bedroom of Shadowitz the black, Philpits the green, and Rosegreen the red. A child asked where the other wizards were.

'The red and green wizards retired some years ago. They decided to go traveling and find places to stay while they did that. They may come back, or maybe not. The black wizard is a rather mysterious and strange fella. He also goes around the land as he pleases. He sometimes comes home in sudden and unexpected times. It's normally just me and Smigerton now, which is very nice, but better when he's not drunk. But he usually is, as he lives in the wine cellar.

'Why does he live down there? One of the boys asked.

'It's the only place he found comfortable without having to use the big staircase. It's also easier for him to help the delivery men when he stays down there. He was a great butler in his day. Now it's a part-time thing. He's close to retirement age anyway.' They then came up to another staircase that spiralled upwards. 'This is the tower that takes you onto the castle roof. That is where I have my big telescope.'

On the roof he showed them his giant telescope. 'I have spent many nights up here, enjoying the wonders that surround us in the night sky. I once saw a witch fly over the moon. Well, she was actually just flying high in the sky but from here it looked like she was over it.'

'Emily's granny is a witch,' said Charlie.

'No, she isn't Charlie! Your mum is a dragon!'

'Now, you kids don't spoil our nice time together and be nice.'

On the observatory walls there were drawings of what Walterwitz had seen through the telescope. There were what looked like planets and stars. Then they saw drawings of stranger-looking shapes. Walterwitz thought they seemed rather puzzled and fascinated by what they saw. He was happy to entertain and amaze them, but also worried about the endless questions that may follow.

'Look at the telescope! It is just wonderful, isn't it? Maybe one night you can come and use it with me. We would see all sorts of things. What do you think Emily?'

'Would we see those things on the wall?'

'We might.'

Emily pointed at one of the strange drawings. 'Is that a giant flying snake?'

'It might be. It is a bit difficult to tell. I think there are all kinds of different animals in life that we don't know about.'

Walterwitz looked at a boy called Billy. 'What would you like to see?'

'I would like to see the snake. Maybe we should shoot it so we can get a good look.'

'Oh, I don't think we should hunt them. They are also very far away. That is the kind of thing Smigerton would like to do, when he isn't drinking. This reminds me, he best do his morning hunting, earlier than usual, as the wine men will be coming tomorrow.'

Walterwitz then showed them his potion room where he makes his magic wands and staffs, as well as some magic powder he had been working on. Holding up a bottle of blue liquid, he then sprinkled some powder into it. The bottle started to glow then grew up to twice its size.

'Now you can taste a drink I've made. It's in the kitchen.' Into the kitchen they went, and there were six glasses of a multi-coloured liquid. They all started to drink up. Then Walterwitz started to think about the time Smigerton mixed the drinks up with potions. The kids all seemed fine, as if they'd only had the drinks. But he suddenly felt like he should take them home.

There was no more to show the children that Walterwitz thought would interest them, so he then started to take them home.

'Wine will be arriving in the morning,' he called out to Smigerton as he opened the door for the kids.

Walterwitz walked all the children to their homes safely and without any trouble. Although, he thought he saw a strange looking shape in the woods, like he was being watched. But, on the way back to the castle, he saw no sign of it again.

Returning to the castle, all was quiet. The door to the cellar was shut, so Smigerton had probably gone to bed early. He probably planned to do a little hunting early in the morning before the wine was delivered.

For a relaxing evening, Walterwitz got out his old sword for sharping and polishing. Smigerton woke up before sunrise and made himself a load of eggs for breakfast. Some were left over, and he left them for Walterwitz. He soon ate up, and sat in his chair for a few minutes to digest. When he felt right, he grabbed his bow and arrows and headed off to the woods. He always felt that if you want to have meat for dinner, you should catch it yourself. It tastes better that way.

Nailed to a tree there was a sign he noticed. It read 'Warning! Suspicious looking strangers about.'

He moved along with his bow in his hand. 'Probably a load of pesky tourists about,' he thought. 'They wouldn't dare get in my way or they'll feel my arrow.'

He stood up against a large tree, with his brown hat, coat and bushy beard, he camouflaged rather well. There was a large hare about. Smigerton then tried to shoot it, but it was too fast for him. He then carried on walking, slowly and carefully. As he looked across, the road that cuts through the trees was visible. Right by it was a deer. It was a perfect shot for him, and he quickly set his bow and arrow ready.

Then it suddenly ran off, and Smigerton saw horses coming along. It was the wine on its way to the castle, given him mixed feelings about what had just happened. Then a bunch of short men with hats, and scarfs around their faces, came out from behind the trees wielding swords. They threw the two delivery men of. Smigerton fired his arrow at them, and it just missed. They saw Smigerton and they all got on the carriage and trotted off through the woods. Smigerton ran over and got just close enough to grab on to the carriage, but it was picking up speed and he hung on for dear life.

The wine men headed to the wizard castle to report the incident to Walterwitz. They told him about some bandits taking the wine, and Smigerton going after them, being dragged through the woods. Walterwitz then grabbed his sword and headed out to where it happened. He let the men rest in the castle.

Once he had found the spot they'd described, he slowly went forward, trying to pick up any clues or traces. He went on for some time through the woods. He had picked up a little scent of Smigerton, but all was rather vague. He just carried on into the woods. He went rather far and thought he was just getting himself lost more than anything.

Finally, he came across a broken crate, with a wine bottle inside. He walked along and found another. There were a lot of rustling noises nearby. He headed over to some huge bushes. Whatever it was, it seemed to be coming out. Maybe it was one of the thieves, or Smigerton, although it seemed like it was something bigger, so Walterwitz had his sword in hand. Then the large dragon head of Crystalex poked out, face to face with Walterwitz.

The dragon seemed surprised to see him. 'What are you doing, old man?'

'I am looking for my friend. He went after some thieves

in the area, and I hope he's not in trouble. What are you doing?'

'I am looking for something I can have for dinner. I haven't had any for three days now.'

'You won't get up to trouble, I hope. I'm sure you get something without that.'

'It doesn't help, you damn humans being so awful. If you need things, they don't just come to you.'

'Well, maybe we can help you. But I must find my fellow Smigerton. Have you not seen any people or white horses around the woods?'

'No.'

Walterwitz then began to sense something, and he excused himself from the dragon. He walked on, and as he did so, he felt that the horse carriage had gone past this way. He started to hear the sound of running horses and the laughter and chatter of men.

'Is this all the wine we have? We haven't had any for weeks!'

'It's the stupid fat fellers fault! He drank some himself and some fell off the cart. I shall deal with him soon.'

The voices were coming from the tent that Walterwitz saw just ahead of him. He carefully sneaked inside without being noticed.

The bandits were there, gathered around a table. He couldn't see what was there or what they were doing. But it didn't matter to him. He was going to teach all these no-good little creeps a lesson.

He stretched out his arms before yelling at them. 'What goes on here?'

They all tried to run and attack, but his magical staff had them dealt with soon enough. They were scattered on the ground around him. On the table he could now see a box that was full of jewels and jewellery. There were also two bottles of wine. He helped himself to some. Then he felt a piece of chain around his neck tighten, making it hard to breath. He tried to grab hold of the chain, but couldn't get a grip. He got out his sword and stuck it into the attacker's leg. He turned around and saw that it was one of the little men. He went out of the tent and left him there.

Smigerton had managed to climb into the carriage, where he then fought with the bandits inside, until one of them smashed a bottle over his head.

He woke up to find himself tied up in some small room. It seemed to be a cave of some kind. He could hear voices and the thud of mugs coming from around the corner. Walterwitz went down a hill at the end of the woods and had a good feeling that he was getting closer to Smigerton.

He came up towards some large rock. Once he past some, he then saw the horses. They were standing outside a doorway in the rock. He tried to listen for anyone about, but all he could hear was the waves of the coast. He went inside, got out his sword, and walked through into an open area.

The bandits were there and soon started to charge at Walterwitz with their swords. One by one, Walterwitz fought them off, as well as all of them together. The wizard proved to be more than a match for them all. Eventually, they gave up. Walterwitz gave them a final glance over, to be sure. He then went down the passage, around the corner he found Smigerton.

'Smigerton, are you all right?'

'I think so. Get me out of here!'

Walterwitz cut the ropes and Smigerton got up to his feet and brushed himself off. They went back to the larger room. The little bandits were gone. Suddenly a giant spider fell down blocking the exit. It started spitting acid at them and little spiders were suddenly running about.

The giant spider moved back and forth. When it got close, Walterwitz swung with his sword, but he missed the spider and it tried spitting back at him. Finally, he managed to slice off one of its legs. It then climbed up on the wall. Smigerton went for the exit, and the spider quickly covered him in cobwebs. Walterwitz went over to cut him free, but the spider threw a load more down on him. The spider went to the other side of the room and climbed down to the ground. Walterwitz and Smigerton tried to get free but the webs were very tough.

Then there was a puff of smoke and Shadowitz was there. With his magic wand, he turned all the spiders, giant and small, to ash. He cut Walterwitz and Smigerton free.

Walterwitz was happy to see him. 'Thank you, friend, I thought we were done for, for a brief moment.'

They went outside, and the bandits were there. Shadowitz and Walterwitz rounded and tied them up.

'Shadowitz, contact the dragon. Tell him I have found dinner for him here.'

Shadowitz did. Crystalex came along and ate the bandits up, then happily returned to his cave.

Walterwitz and Smigerton took the wine to the castle. As they went indoors, Shadowitz and the delivery men were there. Smigerton got a case of wine from the carriage. 'I think we could all do with some of this.'